Naughty!

Caroline Castle & Sam Childs

RED FOX

One afternoon when the sun
began to sink in the sky,
Big Zeb called Little Zeb
to the banana tree.
'Time for bed,
Gorgeous,' she said.
'Cuddle up.'

But Little Zeb wriggled
and giggled and would
not lie down.

'Naughty!'
said Big Zeb.

Little Zeb was not tired.
He threw off his covers and
made a loud noise like an
elephant's trumpet.
'Naughty!' said
Big Zeb.

Big Zeb decided to teach Little Zeb some games to
make him tired.

They played...

Peek-a-boo!

They played...

Whoops-a-daisy!

**Then, as the sun sank lower
in the sky they played...**

Hush-a-bye.

'There,' said Big Zeb. 'There's a sleepy Little Zeb.'
'Where!' cried Little Zeb. 'Where's
a sleepy Zeb?'

'You are,' said Big Zeb dreamily.
'You are my sleepy Little Zeb.'
'Not!' growled Little Zeb.
'Naughty!' said Big Zeb.
And she covered him
up in his blanket
and licked behind
his ear.

Little Zeb lay down
and closed his eyes.
'That's it, Gorgeous,' she
said. 'Tip top.'

Little Zeb made a splash
with his hooves.

At once...

two ears appeared
above the water...

then a nose...

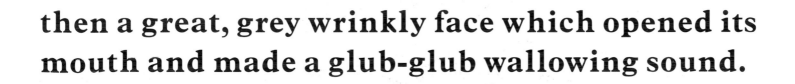

then a great, grey wrinkly face which opened its
mouth and made a glub-glub wallowing sound.

'Peek-a-booOOOOO to you, too!' cried Little Hippo. And he opened his snozzle and snorted a great big fountain at Little Zeb.

'Oooooooo, you naughty!'
cried Little Zeb.
And he splashed
Little Hippo
right back.

Splish!

Splash!

'*You're* the naughty!' snorted Little Hippo.

Splosh!

All of a sudden, the water swirled around in a whirlpool. And from the water rose...

'Whoops-a-daisy!

A big naughty!'

Big Zeb was there
in a flash.

'What's all this splashing?' she said
to Little Zeb. 'You should be in bed.'

'What's all this noise?' said Big Hippo
to Little Hippo. 'You should be in bed.'

'But we're playing,' said Little Hippo.
'Tip top playing,' said Little Zeb happily.

Little Zeb would not go to bed without Little Hippo.
Little Hippo would not go to bed without Little Zeb.

So Big Zeb and Big Hippo wrapped them up
together under the banana tree.
'Hush-a-bye,' whispered Little Zeb.
'Cuddle up.'

As the sun sank even lower in the sky, Big Zeb and
Big Hippo looked at their sleeping babies.

'Who would have thought those two naughties could look so...'

'Gorgeous!' finished Big Zeb.
But...

'Peek-a-boo!' cried Little Hippo.
'Oooo,' cried Little Zeb in delight.
'Tip top naughty!'

For Alison Sage, with love – C.C.
For Francesca Forte, with love – S.C.

A RED FOX BOOK 0 09 941337 X

First published in Great Britain by Hutchinson,
an imprint of Random House Children's Books

Hutchinson edition published 2000
Red Fox edition published 2002

1 3 5 7 9 10 8 6 4 2

Text © Caroline Castle, 2000
Illustrations © Sam Childs, 2000

Red Fox Books are published by Random House Children's Books,
61– 63 Uxbridge Road, London W5 5SA,
a division of The Random House Group Ltd,
in Australia by Random House Australia (Pty) Ltd,
20 Alfred Street, Milsons Point, Sydney, NSW 2061, Australia,
in New Zealand by Random House New Zealand Ltd,
18 Poland Road, Glenfield, Auckland 10, New Zealand,
and in South Africa by Random House (Pty) Ltd,
Endulini, 5A Jubilee Road, Parktown 2193, South Africa

THE RANDOM HOUSE GROUP Limited Reg. No. 954009
www.randomhouse.co.uk

A CIP catalogue record for this book is available from the British Library.

Printed in Hong Kong by Midas Printing Ltd